W9-ABY-988

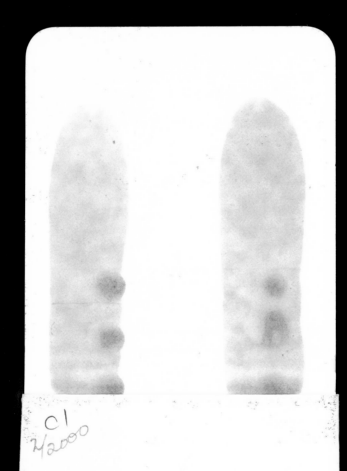

C1
1/2000

PICKERING PUBLIC LIBRARY
CLAREMONT

Hush, Little

For Raleigh, the boy with his head in the stars

Text © 1999 by Daniel Kirk.
Illustrations © 1999 by Daniel Kirk.
All rights reserved. No part of this book may be reproduced or transmitted in
any form or by any means, electronic or mechanical, including photocopying,
recording, or by any information storage and retrieval system, without
written permission from the publisher. For information address
Hyperion Books for Children, 114 Fifth Avenue, New York, New York 10011-5690.

Printed in Hong Kong by South China Printing Company Ltd.
First Edition
1 3 5 7 9 10 8 6 4 2

The illustrations in this book were created using
oil paint on gessoed Strathmore paper.
This book was set in Triplex 45pt.

Library of Congress Cataloging-in-Publication Data
Hush, little alien/by Daniel Kirk; illustrated by Daniel Kirk.
p. cm.
Summary: In this adaptation of the old lullaby, "Hush, Little Baby,"
an extraterrestrial child is promised an assortment of outer space presents
ending with a good night kiss from his adoring father.
ISBN 0-7868-0538-2—ISBN 0-7868-2469-7
1. Folk songs, English—Texts.
[1. Lullabies. 2. Folk songs.] I. Title.
PZ8.3.K6553Hu 1999   [782.42]—dc21 99-10651

**Papa's gonna give you
a kiss good night*!***

And
when
that
rocket
ship
takes
flight,

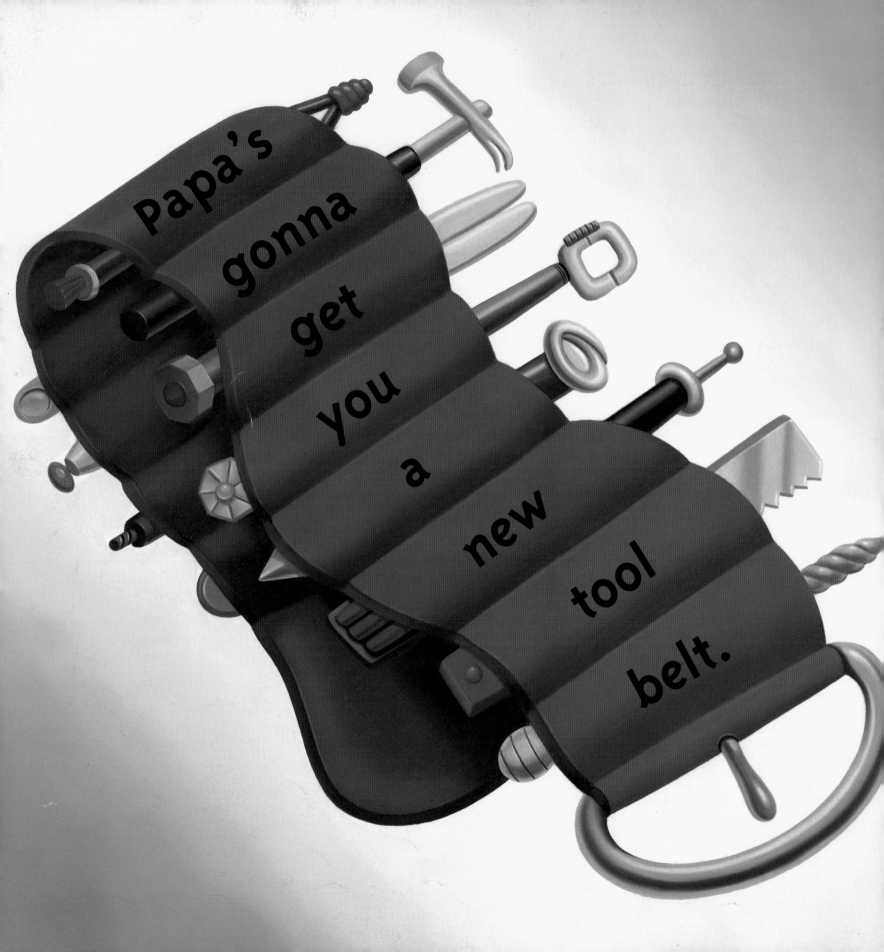

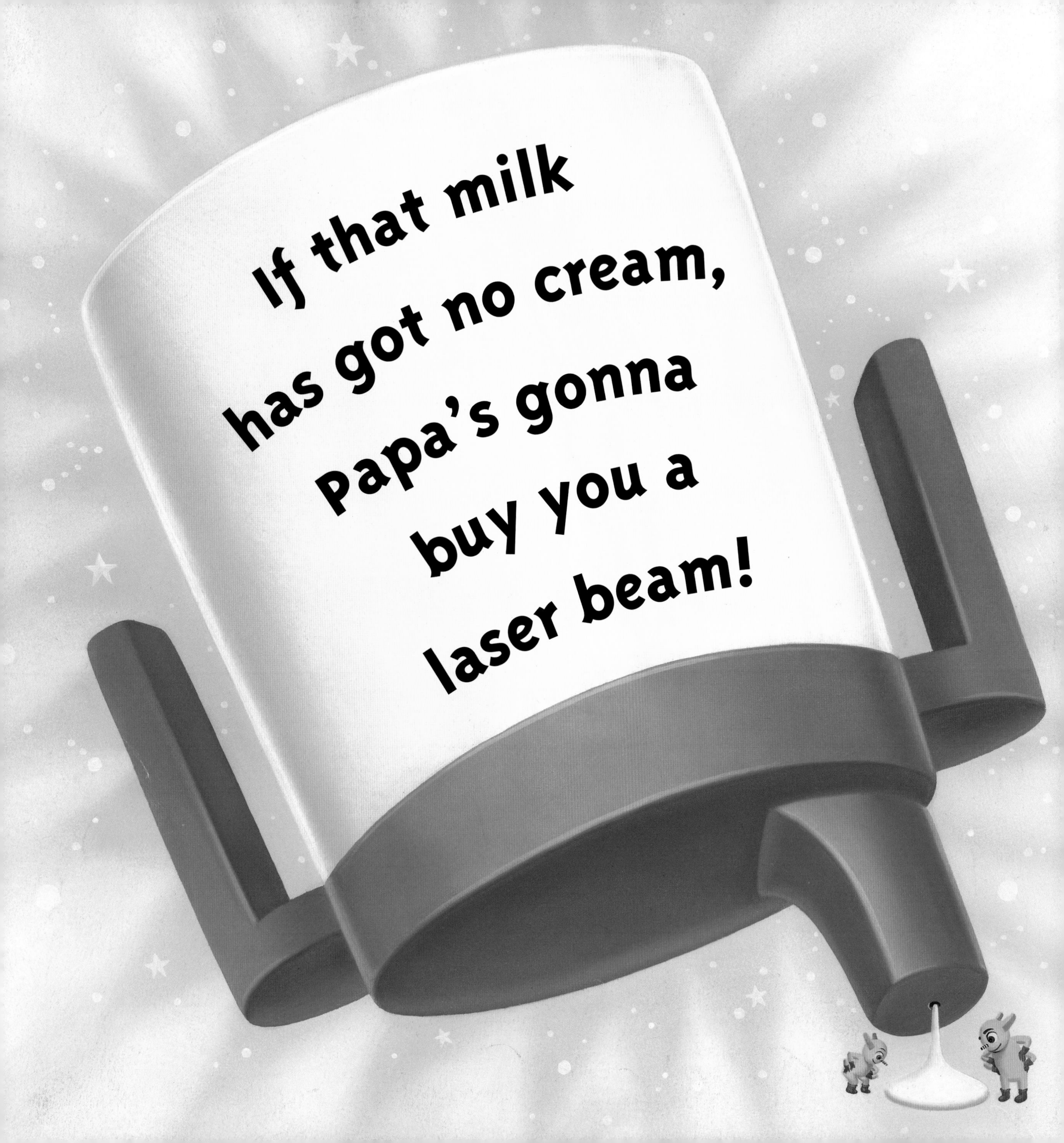

If that milk
has got no cream,
Papa's gonna
buy you a
laser beam!

If that
satellite
gets away,
Papa's gonna
take you to
the Milky Way!

If that astronaut
should fight,
Papa's gonna bring
you a satellite!

If that shooting star's too hot,

Papa's gonna find you an astronaut!

Papa's gonna lasso you a shooting star.

If that goonie bird flies too far,

Papa's gonna catch you a goonie bird.

Hush, little alien,
don't say a word,

5559522

Alien

Daniel Kirk

Hyperion Books for Children • New York